BLACK LEGACY PRESS™

WWW.BLACKLEGACYPRESS.ORG

Octavia
The Octoroon

By
J. F. Lee

ISBN: 978-1-63652-340-8

OCTAVIA

THE OCTOROON

J. F. LEE

CONTENTS

CHAPTER I.
THE PRIZE FIGHT.

Just before the beginning of the civil war between the States there was a large and valuable plantation on the Alabama River on which there were several hundred slaves, said farm being in what is known as the "black belt of Alabama," having a river front of several miles, and annually producing five hundred bales of cotton, fifteen thousand bushels of corn, besides oats, wheat, hay, mules, horses, hogs, cattle, sheep and goats in abundance.

This mammoth farm belonged to Hon. R., then a member of the United States Congress from Alabama, and afterwards a gallant officer in the Confederate army, rising from the rank of first lieutenant to colonel, by which latter title he will be known in this story. He lived in what was then one of the flourishing towns of the State, but which has long since gone to ruin and decay. Colonel R.'s farm was managed by what was then known as an "overseer," but now would be termed a superintendent. He had assistants, white and black, who, with the overseer, managed the farm in a systematic and scientific manner, bringing it up to a high state of cultivation, which made it one of the most productive and valuable in the State.

Colonel R., with his man in livery, a thousand-dollar carriage and finely caparisoned span of horses, visited his farm once a month when at home, to give general directions to his overseer, and receive the annual proceeds of his cotton crop. This was the state of affairs when Lincoln was elected President, when the Southern States seceded from the Union, and when the guns at Fort Sumter belched forth their shot and shell, ushering in a war that had no equal in ancient or modern times.

When the call to arms was made Colonel R. resigned his seat in the Federal Congress, hastened home, raised and equipped a company, which rendered valuable service in the Southern army. Colonel R.'s overseer and his white assistants also responded to the call, joining the company which Colonel R. equipped. Thus was Colonel R.'s farm deprived of white men, and as every able-bodied man was needed at the front, it was out of the question to replace them; nor did he make any effort to do so. However, Colonel R. was not wanting for some one to take charge of his business; he had a quadroon named Simon, who had been carefully trained and drilled by the overseer in farm management. He had been a favorite with the overseer, who made no objection to his fourteen-year-old son teaching him to read and write. He also taught Simon's sister, Elsie. They were both bright quadroons, good looking, and exceptionally intelligent for slaves.

Let me say here that if the planters had any inclination to teach their slaves, the latter had no time but at night to learn, and after working from the time they could see in the morning until they could not see at night, they felt like sleeping when reaching their cabins. However, here and there you would find a negro who could read and write, who generally received such instruction from their owner's or overseer's children.

Simon was twenty-five and Elsie eighteen years of age, both having the same mother, Aunt Dinah, and the same white father.

After the overseer and his assistants left for the army Colonel R. installed Simon as his foreman, with the authority of an overseer. Under his administration farm matters moved along as well as they did under the overseer. In slavery times there was always a negro head man, leader and squire among the negroes, who performed their marriage ceremonies (without license), exhorted at their religious meetings and could sing and pray and be heard a mile. Simon could "out-Herod Herod" in doing all this. He was faithful, honest and upright, three virtues rare among negroes. He successfully kept the farm books, in which were to be recorded the number of pounds of cotton picked per day; the number and weight of each bale of cotton—in a word, this book gave the exact production of the farm, whether it was stock, cotton, corn or what not.

He was provided with a horse and whip, two concomitants that every ante-bellum overseer possessed. Simon felt his importance, and probably was too severe in some instances in using the lash on the slaves. This, however, is characteristic of the negro, as they have since freedom been known to almost whip their children to death. The writer has interfered several times where negro parents were unmercifully chastising their children.

Aunt Dinah, Simon's mother, was rather prepossessing in appearance, and was the plantation mammy, nurse and midwife, as well as the keeper of the orphan asylum for all the little pickaninnies on the plantation. Every place of any size had this character. It is often and truly said that it is the ambition of negro men to be preachers and of the women to be midwives.

Simon had interceded with his master and the overseer to

exempt Elsie from farm work, and to appoint her seamstress, who had several assistants on the farm. She was very apt with the needle and scissors, cutting and making any garment she wished, and doing it all with the needle, this being before the introduction of sewing machines on plantations.

In the eyes of Simon and his mother Elsie was a piece of perfection, a paragon of virtue and chastity, two possessions rare among negroes of both sexes. Elsie was the belle of the plantation, having a large number of suitors, among them two of Colonel R.'s slaves, Brutus and Cæsar.

They were rivals and had an intense hatred for each other on Elsie's account. While Elsie had no idea of accepting either one or any negro, saying that she did not want a "kinky-headed nigger," she encouraged the attentions of both—a consummate flirt, to say the least. Brutus and Cæsar were good specimens of their race, and fairly good looking. Their rivalry increased in intensity and bitterness until they threatened each other's lives.

At this stage of their would-be courtship Simon interfered and told them that, as Elsie was a prize worth contending for, they had to fight a fair fight in the ring, and that he would bestow Elsie upon the victor. The time was appointed for the contest, referees chosen, and all the negroes on the plantation assembled to witness something *à la* Corbett and Fitzsimmons. The battle was fierce, a battle royal; they were contending for the heart and hand of the beautiful Elsie. Neither was able to get the mastery over the other. Both could well say, "Lay on, Macduff! and damned be him who first cries hold, enough!" At times it looked as if Brutus would be victorious, at another, Cæsar.

After they had pounded and bruised each other considerably, and both being well nigh exhausted, the match was called off, and Simon threatened each with a severe lashing if he heard of their fussing any more about Elsie, as she would not marry either one of them. This threat and declaration that Elsie would marry neither embittered the combatants against Simon, both declaring *sotto voce* that they would get even with him yet; that they were as good as he was; that his head was as "kinky" as theirs, and that while they were rivals and personal enemies, they would make common cause against him and kill the bigoted "nigger driver" if he "monkeyed with them."

CHAPTER II.
A BAPTISMAL SCENE.

About a year before this prize fight the "kernel," as his slaves called Colonel R., obtained a furlough to visit his home and plantation. He expressed himself to Simon as being highly pleased at the manner in which he conducted plantation affairs, saying the farm books were neatly kept, stock sleek and fat, cribs full of corn, smoke-houses full of meat, ditches cleaned out, briars kept out of the fence corners—in fact, he saw no difference in his (Simon's) or the overseer's administration, and that he hoped that the work would move along as it was being done at that time. Simon was glad to receive this commendation from his master, and promised that it would be his earnest endeavor to still merit the Colonel's approval.

Colonel R. had been in the army long enough to know that in the end the Confederacy would be beaten; he reasoned that the Southern States were hemmed in by a blockade that no ship of the Confederacy could break, and that they had to depend upon home resources for men, munitions and supplies, while the United States had not only themselves, but the whole world to draw upon. This was good, philosophic reasoning, and he determined to prepare for the collapse, which would be only a question of time. As there was no chance to sell cotton (there being an accumulation of two crops of the fleecy staple, amounting to about a thousand bales, on his place), he gave Simon explicit instructions to hide this cotton if there was any danger of the Federal army raiding that section of the State. He also intrusted to his keeping a large amount of gold which he had hoarded. He told Simon that if he were faithful to the trust he would reward him liberally—that if the Confederacy won he would give him his freedom and $10,000 in gold; and that if the United States won he would still give him the gold named above and make him superintendent on his farm at an annual salary of $2,000. As the sequel will show this compact was faithfully complied with by both parties, and for so doing Simon came near losing his life.

Colonel R. assembled all of his slaves and bade them an affectionate adieu, telling them to be faithful, industrious and diligent, and to be submissive to Simon's authority, and that if he was killed in battle, Mrs. R., his wife and their mistress, would have general supervision of the plantation. He was soon at the front and resumed command of his regiment. Between now and the close of hostilities it will be my endeavor to describe some of the scenes that were enacted on the Colonel's plantation. Elsie was still the belle and had suitors galore.

At every frolic she was the "cynosure of all eyes," the observed of all observers. She never wanted for a partner in the dance or play. Brutus and Cæsar were still rivals and bitter enemies on her account, and at one of the plantation frolics they got into a fight, and Cæsar was killed by Brutus driving an axe into Cæsar's brain. Brutus fled and was a "runaway nigger" until the close of the war.

Simon had a pack of negro dogs which were soon in full cry

on Brutus' track, who ran to the river and went up a tree bending over the water. The dogs were soon there and "treed" Brutus. Simon shortly arrived on the spot, thinking the dogs had Brutus up the tree. The dogs were there, the tree was there, and no doubt Brutus went up the tree, but he was not there. Simon gave up the chase, declaring that a negro who was sharp and strategical enough to climb a tree, and then jump into the river and swim across, would no doubt outwit the dogs, were he to take them across and continue the pursuit.

Elsie was thus relieved of her two most importunate and troublesome suitors—one dead and the other in the woods.

A negro is intensely religious, regardless of honesty and integrity; he will attend night services, shout, sing and pray, and then return home by some hen-roost and lift off a chanticleer which has been doing business at that stand for a half dozen years with as much nonchalance as if he, "Cuffee," were eating his dinner or taking a drink of water.

On this plantation there were two rival churches, Methodist and Baptist, and I would say here that, as a rule, Southern negroes belong to one or the other of these two large branches of the Christian Church.

During the summer these two churches held revival (and rival) services every night and Sunday for three or four weeks, at which there was a great awakening and a large ingathering of souls to the flock. For some reason it is thought the Methodist "nigger" can shout, sing and pray louder than his Baptist brother, while the latter can head him off in drinking whisky, which is counteracted by the Methodist brother's love for chickens and turkeys and their proclivities for lifting them off the roost.

At one of these night services, when everybody was happy,

shouting, singing and praying, and the house was in an uproar and it seemed that pandemonium had turned loose, a large lighted lamp full of oil was turned over and exploded.

Negroes piled out of the windows and doors by the dozens. Some of the cooler heads pulled off their coats, and wrapping up the burning negroes, finally subdued the flames. Order was finally restored and all assembled again in the house. The pastor in charge then arose and said: "My bredderin an' sisterin, we is all run a narrer resk in bein' burn to deth, an' it shood be a terrible warnin' tu perpare for de burnin' dat awaits de ongodly, an' ef de richous am skasely saved whar shall de sinner an' ongodly appeer? Brudder Sam, you is de wus burnt nigger hear tu-nite, an' ef you keep on stealin' chickens you is gwine to go whar de wurm dieth not an' de fire is not squinched."

At this eloquent appeal on the part of the pastor moans and groans were heard all over the house, that have to be heard to be realized. Old Sister Ann, a two-hundred-and-fifty-pounder, got happy and began throwing her hands in the air, and popping them together, shouting, "Glory! Glory!" and started towards the pastor, saying, "Brudder Zeke, I'm so happy I wants tu hug you!" whereupon she gathered him, a weak man, in her herculean arms. He began to struggle to free himself from her vise-like grasp—she was about to squeeze the life out of him—but in vain! He then shouted for some one to "take her off! take her off!" Several of the brethren interfered and finally released the struggling pastor. After which he said: "Sister Ann, de wedder is tu hot, soap is tu scase, an' you is tu big an' fat tu git close to ennybody; so pleas kep yo' distunce."

Brother "Zeke," fearing a similar experience, announced services for the following night, and immediately dismissed the congregation. On the last Sunday of the meeting baptismal services were held at both churches, the Baptists assembling at the river to perform the rite by immersion, and the Methodists at their church to perform it by sprinkling or pouring.

At the latter church the pastor requested all the converts, which were fifty or sixty, to come forward to receive baptism, whereupon about a dozen responded. He stated that only about a fourth of the converts had come forward, and that if the rest were in the house they will now come forward and be baptized.

The preacher replied that he was very liberal in his views, and that he would baptize by sprinkling, pouring or immersion, and for each applicant to designate the mode, and it would be carried out. Those who had not come forward said that they "wanted tu go under de water." He said they would go to the river just as soon as he got through with those present. Whereupon those who had come forward told the preacher that as he had to go into the water they would be immersed also. The minister then announced for the congregation to assemble on the river to witness the baptisms. The Baptist and Methodist preachers reached the water about the same time, and after conferring with one another, agreed that the order would be for one minister to baptize one of his flock and the other one, and so on, alternately, until they were through. This took some time, as each had about fifty apiece to baptize. There was shouting and rejoicing during this baptismal scene. There were probably two thousand negroes present, those on adjoining plantations also being present. It is a fact that baptism in water will draw almost as large a crowd as a circus.

With the exception of shouting on the part of converts there was no noise or disturbance, and all went well until the last, the baptism of a large, fleshy sister, who, as she arose from the water clapped her hands and shouted: "I see my Jesus!" When she said this a negro, who had climbed into a willow tree leaning over the water, replied: "Yu lie, yu hypercritical old huzzie; tain't nuthin' but a snappin' mud turcle yu seed, an' hit's a pity he hadn't kotched yu by de nose an' drowned yu, so as yu would not tell lies enny more on 'spectable niggers." As he said this the tree broke, precipitating him into water twenty feet deep, and as he could not swim he went straight to the bottom. Both of the parsons were silent spectators of this last act, and were making for the shore as the congregation sang "Pull for the Shore." They had been fishers, as it were, of souls; now that an opportunity presented itself, they in reality would have to be fishers of men—at least one would have to be. The Methodist, thinking the Baptist more used to water than he, waited for the Baptist to strike out for the drowning man, and the Baptist did the same for the Methodist. The latter, seeing that the man would drown if no assistance were rendered, and being the nearest, swam to him. The drowning man grabbed him around the waist and both sank. The Baptist parson, being in the water, thought he was duty bound to render assistance, and swam to the scene just as they arose, when the Methodist grabbed the Baptist around the waist, and all three went under together. Things were getting serious, as it would be the third time the man went under. One of the men on shore succeeded in time to catch the first man, who was sinking the last time, by the hair, and by superhuman jerks released him from the parson and succeeded in carrying him to the shore. As this was being done another negro on shore swam and caught the exhausted Methodist parson by the wool, jerking him off from the Baptist, and carried him to shore. Another wicked negro on the bank shouted: "Fair play; I'll be darned if the Baptis' shell drown," and made for him, catching him by his cue and landing him safely on land. The congregation could have consistently sung, during the last three acts, "Pull for the Shore." As the submerged negroes were resting one skeptical darky shouted out, "You's all Baptis' now." Thus ended this baptismal and almost tragical scene.

CHAPTER III.

THE BIRTH OF OCTAVIA.

Not long after this Simon's mother, Aunt Dinah, "went the way of all the earth, and was gathered to her fathers." This caused great mourning and lamentation on the plantation. The old auntie was almost looked upon with reverence. She was, as it were, an oracle, being consulted on everything that transpired on the place.

This was a severe grief to Simon and Elsie, who received the condolences of all the slaves on the place. The little negroes were bereft of a true friend, as Aunt Lucy, Aunt Dinah's successor, was not as thoughtful, good and kind to the little ones as Aunt Dinah had been.

The negro is no nurse and of no account in a sick room. This was so in the case of the deceased old auntie, who was sick quite awhile and doubtless wanted good nursing. But let one of their number die and they are very much in evidence, sitting up with the corpse or attending the funeral. Aunt Dinah had one of the longest funeral processions ever witnessed in that country.

The negroes not only preach at the burial, but appoint a time several months ahead, giving it great publicity, when So and So's funeral will be preached with great *éclat*. On these occasions there is as much shouting, singing, groaning, moaning and praying as there is in their revival meetings.

Simon and Elsie put on the usual mourning for parents, and to show their grateful remembrance asked their mistress to get them an elegant monument, with the proper inscription thereon, and erected it at the head of her grave, something very rare for slaves.

Soon after this Elsie got in bad health, would not eat, and notwithstanding much was done for her restoration to health, she failed to improve. The negro as a race has a larger share of superstition than any other. With this Simon was considerably tinctured. As Elsie failed to improve it was noised around that she was "conjured." Simon, notwithstanding his intelligence, began to share in the belief that this was so. There was an old negro "conjure" doctor on the place, whom Simon asked to go around and see Elsie.

After talking with Elsie awhile he left, and seeing Simon told him that "Elsie grievin' 'bout Brutus." He protested that she cared nothing in the world about that negro in the woods, and he would have to search for another cause. Believing that she was "conjured," he insisted that the conjurer take the "spell" off. To this he agreed, and appointed a day when he would bring her around all right. The "conjurer" told Simon that Elsie had "lizards and roaches" in her ear, and that they must come out. It is possible that Simon believed this stuff by letting his superstition get the better of his judgment and intelligence. At the appointed time the "conjurer" came, having lizards and roaches in a box up his sleeve. After songs, incantations and gesticulations, all the while rubbing her head, he adroitly liberated the lizards and roaches, which ran off, making Elsie scream. This may have had effect on the few spectators present, but it certainly had none on Elsie, who knew that she had been acting a piece of consummate duplicity from the first. The "conjurer" told Elsie, "dem live things in her hed wus de cause of all her trubble, and that she would get well now." Elsie, however, failed to improve, and Simon went to see his mistress in regard to the matter, who sent a physician back with him to see Elsie. When leaving he told Simon that Elsie had given birth to a beautiful girl baby as white as he, the physician, was, and with hair as straight.

Horror of horrors! This was "the unkindest cut of all." Simon was crushed, humiliated, and felt that he was disgraced by the conduct of his sister; and to think of her duplicity for all those months was enough to cause an angel to swear. He and his sister were the most intelligent and refined negroes in all that country. They were the *élite*, the bon ton, the upper crust, and were looked on as such by the other slaves. If there were aristocrats among slaves, Simon and sister filled the bill. Simon had held his sister up to the negro girls on the place as an example, and for her to bring disgrace on them in that way was too much!

Aunt Lucy, Elsie's nurse, said that Elsie had no ordinary baby; that "it was white as the whitest, eyes as blue as ole mars'er, an' hair as strate as ole missis, an' not a white man in de kentry. Dis weren't no nigger baby; Elsie she got wid chile by de Holy Spirit." Simon knew that the days of miracles had passed, and that none other than a white man was its father. Elsie admitted after a long time that her owner was the child's father. Whether he was satisfied, Simon said no more about it, but refused for a long while to even see the baby. Time heals all things, and finally Simon consented to see it and was struck with her beauty. Elsie named her child Octavia, and as it grew in years Simon began to love the child as his own. She became a favorite on the whole plantation, nothing being too good that any of the slaves had for little Octavia. She was a heroine from the first, as she proved to be in after life.

To all appearances she was as pure as the purest Caucasian, and if an expert had been put on the stand to swear as to her race he would have said Caucasian. Such are the circumstances under which this afterwards wonderful being was brought into existence.

With a white father and quadroon mother, this made her seven-eighths Caucasian.

CHAPTER IV.

ALMOST A WATERY GRAVE.

Before proceeding further I would say that the standard of virtue among the negroes is very low, and that if any of their girls wander from the paths of virtue they are not cast off as is the case with the whites. It must be admitted, however, that there is an improvement among them along this line. When Octavia was a year old she came very near being drowned in the river. Elsie was fond of fishing, and carried Octavia and a little negro nurse to watch the child. The nurse got careless and let the child fall into the river, and would have drowned had not Simon happened to be near and heard his sister's screams, and getting there, jumped in just in time to rescue both mother and child, the former having leaped in to save the child. Simon gave his sister a good lecture and the nurse a switching for their carelessness. It seemed that Simon's nearness was providential.

Simon always said, after the child was a few months old, that she had a bright future before her; that, though a slave, the Lord would open up a way for her.

In Colonel R.'s absence Simon was required to make frequent visits to his mistress's home to report to her the progress he was making on the farm. The war had been over half fought, and while the Confederacy had gained many battles it suffered serious losses, and was daily getting weaker, and it was only a question of time when it would collapse. During his visits to his mistress Simon gained this intelligence in regard to the progress of the war, and while he was sure of his freedom, regardless of the way the war terminated, he could not but wish for the success of the Union armies on account of his sister and her child, who would thereby gain their freedom. He also had a broad, sympathetic feeling for his race and wanted them liberated.

He was also broad enough in his philosophy and intelligence to accord to his master and other Southern slaveholders the right to resort to arms to fight for property which they had bought or inherited, and which was recognized in the Constitution of the United States.

While he was legally a slave he enjoyed freedom as much so as his master or other white men. He had all the comforts of a country home, and while the large plantation over which he was foreman was not his, he was in one respect "lord of all he surveyed." He had a buggy, horse, saddle, whip, pack of hounds, and said to this, do so and so, and it was done; or go and they came or went. When one of the slaves transgressed he used the lash on him—in a word, he was as supreme in authority as the Nabob of Cawnpore or the Sultan of Turkey. Enjoying and having all these things at his command, why should he want them terminated? It must be remembered that he was three-fourths white, and one of the instincts of the Anglo-Saxon is freedom and liberty. Simon was attached to his master and mistress, who were humane, kind and thoughtful of their slaves. Still, with all this, there was a longing in his heart that would not be satisfied. It is admitted on all sides that had there not been cruel and heartless slaveholders, "Uncle Tom's Cabin" would never have been written, sympathy in Northern pulpits and Abolition societies would not have spread, and in all probability the negro would yet have been a slave. Simon's reasoning was that he nor his master were responsible for human slavery, which in some respects had been a benefit and in others an injury to the negro, and that there had been slavery in all ages of the world.

He knew that the mistake was made when slavery was recognized in the Constitution of the United States; also that the mistake had brought the negro from the wilds of Africa, and civilized, tamed and made a good laborer and citizen of him. That was the entering wedge which had caused all the contention, and finally precipitated the most gigantic war in history.

Let the consequences be what they may, Simon did his duty in successfully managing the affairs on his master's plantation.

CHAPTER V.
THE "UNDERGROUND RAILWAY."

While he did nothing openly to oppose the Confederacy, he aided in a secret way the escape of his sister and niece.

Simon was not absolutely certain of the success of the Union armies, and to insure the freedom of his sister and niece, he made use of the first opportunity, which soon presented itself. As is well known, there was before the war what was known as an "Underground Railway" for the escape of slaves to the free States and Canada. This was nothing more nor less than agents sent out by Northern Abolition societies to abduct slaves, thousands of whom escaped in this manner.

It was on this account that the "Fugitive Slave Law" was passed by Congress, on which there was the test case before the Supreme Court in the slave, Dred Scott, said court sustaining the law. One of the Northern societies at this time sent an agent South as a spy, and to abduct any slave or slaves that he could entice away. This agent made his way to Colonel R.'s plantation, over which Simon was foreman. He cautiously made known his business to Simon, who welcomed and secretly harbored him. This agent was joined two days after by an escaped Union soldier from the Confederate prison at ——. This was a happy and unexpected meeting between the spy and soldier. What they did had to be done quickly and secretly. If they were captured the spy would be executed and the soldier reincarcerated in prison. Simon also had enemies on the farm who would give him away to the nearest provost marshal if it was known that he was harboring these men. Simon arranged for an immediate conference at night, when it was agreed upon that they were to take Elsie and Octavia, and for two stout negro men to go also, to alternately carry Octavia, who by this time was a year and a half old and full grown for her age. Simon spotted two stout negro men whom he thought he would have no trouble in getting to go along. But the very first one he approached, named Henry, bluntly and insolently refused. Simon told him then that if he ever divulged it he would handle him roughly. Henry left, telling him to "go on 'bout his biziness; that he fixin' tu git hisself in trubble." He had no trouble in getting the next he approached, whose names were Jim and Jack.

All necessary arrangements being made, they assembled at the gin house on the night of departure to bid Simon farewell. He parted with his sister with many misgivings, fearing that she might lose her own and the baby's life in this attempt to escape. He bade each man adieu, and Elsie and Octavia an affectionate farewell. He returned home, retired, but there was no sleep for him that night. At times he was almost tempted to pursue the escaping party and bring them back. Without Elsie and the child he was indeed desolate, as he had not a single relation in all that country. Just before day he managed to fall asleep, to be awakened almost immediately by a commotion in the negro quarter, and on inquiring the cause was told that Jim and Jack had run away.

He then told his informant that Elsie and Octavia could not be found, and they must have been stolen by the negro men. To allay suspicion he had his horse saddled, blew up his dogs, and was soon ostensibly on the negroes' tracks. He took pains however, to go in a different direction to the one the escaping party went. After making a spurious chase of three or four hours he returned, saying that the negroes had escaped, at the same time making loud lamentations because Elsie and the child had been stolen. It is unnecessary to say that his grief was real.

Let us now follow the fugitives. They traveled only at night, concealing themselves in the day.

The second night out they met some one with a squealing pig on his shoulder. The Northerners, fearing detection, captured the man, who proved to be Brutus, the runaway negro from Colonel R.'s farm. They explained their mission to him, and asked him to go along with them, and if he didn't they would treat him like he was going to treat that stolen pig, which he took out of the pen up the road. Elsie being in the party, he was only too glad to accompany them. He proved to be a valuable acquisition, being used to the woods, detecting any noise with the celerity of a cat. He was also of great assistance in carrying Octavia, considering it a labor and burden of love, and would not relinquish her, only from sheer exhaustion.

All went well with the party, until the fourth night out, when they came to a swollen river, and not a skiff to be found. An axe had been brought along, to use in such a contingency, with which a raft was soon made, and the party on it, and was being rowed over by the negroes, who were three-fourths across, when, by some unaccountable manner, Octavia fell overboard, and would have been drowned if the moon had not been shining, which gave light for Brutus, who had jumped in the river, to see and catch her as she arose, when he swam to the shore with her.

It seemed that fate was against the little child, this being the second time in her brief existence that she had narrowly escaped a watery grave. The day after this accident they came near being detected, but, through the strategy of Brutus, they escaped.

Two more nights brought them in hearing of the opposing armies, and to pass the Confederate sentinels was the "tug of war." They decided, however, to make the attempt, rather than make a circuit of seventy-five miles to flank the Southern lines. On the night the attempt was made it was dark, and all would have been well if Octavia had not cried out when passing the last sentinel. At this the whole party rushed past, the sentinel firing several times into the party, killing Jim and Jack, and wounding Octavia seriously and Elsie slightly. The Northerners and Brutus escaped to the Union army. Elsie and child were carried to the Confederate headquarters and had their wounds examined and dressed. The surgeon said Elsie was all right, but that it would take good nursing and skillful treatment for the child to pull through. But she did, and when able to travel they were put on a horse in charge of a squad of soldiers, with authority to investigate the circumstances of their escape as soon as they reached Colonel R.'s plantation. Henry became alarmed, turned State's evidence against Simon, who, without time to exchange words of greeting with Elsie and the child, was hurried off and put in the county jail, and was succeeded as foreman by Henry, who probably had this in view when he gave Simon away. This was another crushing blow to Simon; this was capping the climax. What, Colonel R.'s handsome and intelligent foreman in jail? This was indeed humiliating! Simon's enemies on the farm were now elated because of his downfall. One ancient son of Ham, who had been lashed severely for his misconduct by Simon, soliloquized thus: "Dey sho' is got dat yaller son of a b—— now; he tink he white, but I'll be goldurn my black skin ef dey doan salt an' tan his yaller hide an' make it look yallerer dan 'tis." Simon could think of no way of getting relief. While he had been faithful to the trust which his master had confided in him, and who might be willing to forgive him, yet he knew his master was powerless to get him out of jail, he being in the conspiracy in abducting his master's slaves, and of feeding and harboring a spy. However, he wrote to his master, making full confession, and begged forgiveness, and asked him if there was any way possible for him to get out of prison. But before the letter reached the front there had been a battle, and Colonel R. had been captured and was a prisoner on Johnson's Island. The letter was returned unopened. He considered his last ray of hope gone, if hope it was, as he was almost certain that his master could afford no relief. He endeavored to compose himself the best he could; he was visited frequently by Elsie and Octavia. She upbraided herself to Simon as being the cause of it all. He asked her not to do that, as he blamed no one but himself. On her first visit he sent a letter to his mistress, giving explicit instructions and information where the treasure was which his master had confided to his keeping. Simon being in jail, she sent and had it brought home, and found every cent as the Colonel had left it.

Elsie kept Simon supplied with papers, books, and such delicacies as the distracted state of the country would admit of.

CHAPTER VI.

MISTAKEN IDENTITY AND ESCAPE FROM BRUIN.

While he was whiling away the weary hours in jail another scene was being enacted at the plantation. Railroads were not as fashionable and plentiful as now, and had not driven the boats from the river, on which was a magnificent line of steamers which plowed the waters from Mobile to Montgomery. They were veritable floating palaces, and were the admiration of all. The writer of this, though in middle life, never tires looking at a fine steamer or train of cars. This was so of Elsie, who frequently went to the plantation landing, carrying Octavia with her.

At this time a magnificent side-wheel steamer had been built, and was advertised to leave Mobile at a certain time, and would pass the landing on Colonel R.'s farm at noon.

About six months previous to this a prominent lady living in Mobile had had her three-year-old daughter, named Octavia, stolen from her. Strenuous efforts were made to find her, large rewards being offered for her return, but in vain! This lady had a brother, a captain in the Southern army, who had been on duty at Mobile. He assisted his sister in her efforts to find her child, to whom he had become much attached. This captain and his company were transferred to another part of the Confederacy, and took passage on this boat, he telling his almost crazed sister that he would keep a sharp lookout for her child.

The boat arrived at the landing at the appointed time, and stayed there some time to put off a lot of freight. Among the spectators on the bank were Octavia and her mother. This army captain saw Octavia and thought he saw a resemblance to his sister's lost child. He told some of his company to accompany him ashore, and as soon as he was in speaking distance he was sure he had found the lost child, and running to the child took her in his arms, exclaiming, "My Octavia, my long-lost child," at the same time kissing and caressing her. Elsie, dumfounded with fear, began crying, and told the captain that the child's name was Octavia, but that she was its mother. The captain threatened to have her arrested by his soldiers if she didn't hush up. The captain of the boat saw and heard it all. Elsie by this time was yelling and screaming at the top of her voice, and was trying to take the child from the captain, who ordered his soldiers to take Elsie. By this time the captain of the boat had arrived at the scene, and suggested to the army captain that it was possible for him to be mistaken, and that this child may be his sister's child's double. He told Elsie to send for her witnesses, which she did, and soon had a dozen negroes of the place who positively identified the child as being Elsie's. Among the witnesses was Aunt Lucy, who was Elsie's nurse at the birth of the child in the captain's arms, who had been struggling to get out. This was positive proof, and the captain gave her back, saying this was a clear case of mistaken identity, and as he was honestly mistaken he would make the *amende honorable*.

Aunt Lucy said: "Dunno what gwine cum of dat chile; she been drowned twice, an' kilt wunst wid de soljer's gun, an' now dis Mister Cap'n tink she his sister loss chile. Sho', 'fore Gawd, dis nigger dunno what gwine cum to dat chile. Elsie better take her hoam an' keep her dar." Elsie gathered the child in her arms, crying and shouting for joy, at this narrow escape of again losing her child.

All of this was reported to Simon, who ordered his sister to stay at home and keep the child there with her. This was carried out to the letter, and deprived her of the pleasure of seeing Simon; but better that than run the risk of losing her child.

In the earlier days of Alabama the forests were full of game of all kinds, bears being plentiful at one time. They were very destructive to the farmers' calves, lambs and pigs, and, in a few instances, to children. A determined war had been made upon them and most of them had been destroyed, but, as we will see, there was at least one left, as one actually came out of the swamp to the Colonel's negro quarters, and attacked Elsie's child, and would have killed her but for her and the other children's screams, which attracted the dogs and some men near, the latter gathering clubs, axes or anything at hand, and with the dogs' help finally dispatched him, but not before he had killed one of the dogs. Bruin was probably no respecter of persons, and attempted to appropriate the prettiest child he could find. After this Aunt Lucy said: "My Gawd, what nex'? De 'Federate cap'n like got her, an' now a big ole b'ar. I 'spec he hongry, an' want white chile to smack he mouf on." Elsie was indeed grateful that her child had escaped this awful death. It was her daily prayer that no evil should befall her child. While the means of rescue had always heretofore been at hand, it might not be so in the future.

The war between the States dragged heavily on—at one time the Northern and at another the Southern armies were successful. Colonel R. languished in a Northern prison on Johnson's Island, while Simon did the same thing in a county prison in Alabama.

The Confederate States were strongly blockaded, so much so that there could be no egress nor ingress except by blockade runners, which was a dangerous piece of business. Consequently very few of the delicacies of life could be had in the Southern States. This blockade also kept out quinine, which is so necessary in the South. For the want of this Octavia came near dying from an attack of malarial fever. Her physician gave her up to die, telling the attendants there was no hope for her. She lay unconscious for days, and it seemed as if every breath would be her last. During this stage of her illness it was suggested that an all-night prayer-meeting be held in her behalf. Being a favorite, the negroes turned out *en masse*, Octavia's only attendants were her mother and Aunt Lucy.

They carried their devotions on all night, singing, moaning, groaning and praying, and were too much exhausted to do anything the next day. At one time during the night Aunt Lucy said to Elsie that the child was surely dead. But by close examination Elsie said she could detect a weak, thready pulse at the wrist, and slight movement of the chest, and said that "while there is life there is hope." Still she was cold half way up her extremities, and the two were kept busy making hot applications. She lay in this condition two days after the prayer-meeting. Finally she said in the faintest whisper that she wanted some water, and from then began to improve, and in a month was playing with the other children.

Aunt Lucy always said that "dem niggers brought dat chile fru by dey prars. De Scripters say, 'de ferbent, effectual prar of de richus availeth much, an' de prar ob faith shel' save de sick.'"

There was much rejoicing because of Octavia's recovery, and none rejoiced more than Elsie, who thought her and the negroes' prayers were answered.

While on the subject of having prayer-meeting for any special object, I will relate the following incident: In a certain section of country there was a drouth of long standing prevailing, and it looked as if everything would be parched up, and nothing be saved for man or beast. It was suggested that the negroes have a prayer-meeting at their church to bring rain. One of my neighbors, who was almost a skeptic, encouraged the negroes, most of whom farmed on the large plantation which he owned. On the appointed night there was a large crowd present, who prayed, sang and shouted until three o'clock in the morning, when there came up one of the most terrific storms which that section had ever experienced. It rained a perfect flood; the wind was a most frightful tornado, tearing down houses, fences, crops, trees, and killing some stock. The hail was terrific, ruining some crops. My neighbor met some of the brethren the next day and said: "Boys, what made you pray so hard last night? We wanted rain, and not a h—l of a storm like we got." One of them replied: "Boss, I tells you how it wuz. Dat fool nigger Pascal was de cause of de whole ting. In his prayer las' nite he prayed de Lawd not to sen' one of dem leetle drizzle-drazzle showers, but one of dem trash movers. An', boss, we sho' got it, an' mo' too. I tell you, boss, dem niggers prayed all nite for rain, an' when it did cum yu jes' ought tu seen dem niggers prayin' fur de rain, win' an' hail tu stop. We thought sho' we gwine git kilt. Dat fool nigger Pascal got no sence nohow; we keeps him home de nex' time we wants rain."

In commemoration of Octavia's restoration to health the negroes appointed a day of thanksgiving and prayer. The negro is nothing if not religious; he can surpass his white brother two to one in fervency and zeal, but whether that "zeal is according to knowledge" is not my province to decide. It is the custom of the negroes in their religious meetings to line out their hymns for singing, and when at their work you can hear them repeat two lines, sing it, and the other two lines to make out the verse, and sing that. It is a rare thing to see a skeptical negro of the Ingersoll type. I have already said something about superstition; this characteristic, like religion, is developed to a high degree. If one starts anywhere and forgets something, on going back he makes a cross mark and spits in the mark. If one starts on a journey and a rabbit crosses the road before him, he turns around and goes back home. If one is sick and a screech owl screams near by, the sick person is sure to die. One could not be hired to go in a cemetery by himself at night. When any one dies they can see his "sperit" going about the place. They are strong believers in ghosts and "sperits." These and many other superstitions render them difficult patients to treat. The writer was called to see a sick negro on one occasion, and could not find that there was anything the matter with him. In my examination I found a bag the size of one's fist tied under his shirt. I drew it out and asked what it was. He would make no reply, when an old granny, who was nurse, said that was his "conjure" bag to keep "sperits" off with. It contained rags, rocks, gourd seed, a hog tusk and a tack.

CHAPTER VII.
LIBERATED.

After Octavia's restoration to health she looked prettier than ever. Her beauty and intelligence were proverbial, and drew spectators from many miles away. There was so much said about the matter that Elsie's mistress made a special visit to see the child, who was now between four and five years old. Whether she "smelled a mouse" or not is not known, but certain it is that she entered into negotiations with a party in the adjoining county to sell Elsie and child to him. He first hesitated, fearing that the negro's mistress did not have the legal right to sell them. He consulted an attorney, and found that anything of the kind done by Colonel R.'s wife in his absence would stand good in law. With this advice he bought Elsie and Octavia. Simon heard of this and was hurt by it very much. Still, they were not very far off, and that was much better than if they had been sent out of the State. Her new owner, however, did not own her long, as we shall see.

We have now arrived at that period when there was great consternation and despair on the part of the white people of the country. It was reported far and near that Gen. Wilson, one of the Union generals, was making a raid through central Alabama with a large army. Simon heard of this and knew that he would soon be liberated from prison. He had, however, hidden Colonel R.'s cotton where he was sure it could not be found. The report about General Wilson's raid proved to be true, as a detachment went through the town where Simon was confined, and turned all the prisoners out. Simon hastened home, and the first person he saw was Henry, who fled on sight, fearing that Simon would do him harm for turning State's evidence against him. A detachment of the army went through the county that Elsie was carried to, taking all the stock and negro men with them. Knowing that Simon had been liberated and was at home, she and Octavia left immediately to join him, and arrived about sunset the following day. This was a happy meeting between the three. Elsie had had no opportunity to have private conversation with him since she was brought back by the Confederate soldiers, when they started on the "Underground Railway" for freedom. Consequently she had much to tell him about that trip, and of her brief sojourn in the adjoining county. They conversed far into the night, and finally went to sleep wondering what would be next on the docket. They didn't have to wonder long, as by some means never known Henry had found out about Colonel R. intrusting a large amount of gold with Simon, and when he fled at Simon's appearance, he went immediately to the Federal General's headquarters and reported this fact.

Henry thought there might be dollars in his pocket by giving this news. He gave a detailed account of the matter, telling about Simon being a "nigger driver," having a pack of "nigger dogs," and being heartless and cruel to the hands on the place. He endeavored to incense the commander as much as possible against Simon. The General sent a captain with a company of soldiers to see if there was anything in Henry's report. On the way Henry urged the captain to hang Simon. Of course he wanted this done as a protection to himself, as he well knew that Simon would handle him roughly if he got his hands on him, because he, Henry, had given him away.

On arriving at the plantation Simon was immediately arrested and asked where the gold was. Simon said he once knew, but didn't then, which was true, as his former mistress had had it moved. Henry shouted that "Simon was lying." The captain informed him that he had orders to hang him if he did not divulge the whereabouts of the gold. He still protested that he knew nothing about it then. The captain ordered him tied, amid the screams of Elsie and Octavia. Simon then tried to reason with the captain, telling him of harboring the Union spy and the escaped soldier; of his planning the escape of Elsie, Octavia, Jim and Jack; of Henry's refusal to go, and that he was the one that ought to be hung. Henry hollered out, "He's a liar; I wanted to go and he wouldn't let me." The captain said he had to execute his orders, and ordered Simon taken to the nearest tree, when Octavia, giving a loud scream, fell on her knees before the captain (who reined his horse up), exclaiming, "Oh, Mister Taptain, pease don't hang Uncle Simon; he ain't done nothin'!"

The captain thought he had never seen a lovelier object in his life, and his heart, that had probably been hardened by a four years' war, was touched. That beautiful, kneeling child, with streaming locks and eyes of heavenly blue, and cheeks like a ripe peach, was enough to melt a heart of stone. He dismounted and gathered the child in his arms, caressing and kissing her, saying that she was exactly like his little Octavia at home. He drew a picture from his pocket of his child, and it proved to be the image of this child. He told Octavia that he would release her uncle. She showed her appreciation by caressing the captain, who ordered all the stock on the place, with negro men on them, to be carried off. Whether they really intended to hang Simon is not known, but certain it is that several slaveholders were hung about that time to extort from them the whereabouts of hidden treasure. This was done by the ex-slaves, probably mostly for revenge. But it is to the honor of the Union soldiers that they did not countenance any such action, and in some instances rescued the parties from a probable death. This revenge was to be expected, as most any race, after being in bondage a hundred years or more, if left to themselves and had the power, would do the same.

There was great lamentation on the part of the negro men's wives when their husbands left. Simon, Elsie and Octavia were the only composed ones on the place. Simon assured them that all of them would soon be back.

After this wholesale foraging of negroes and stock, things indeed looked desolate. The crop had been planted, good stands obtained; it had been worked once and was very promising. But under the present status of affairs it was out of the question to try and work it. Simon and Elsie, however, did not despair. Both had been raised to work, knew how, and could do so again. The oxen on the plantation had been unmolested, a yoke of which were pressed into service, Simon doing the plowing and Elsie the hoeing. In a few days the negroes who had been carried off began to come in, until about all had returned. Simon advised each to harness up the oxen on the place and plow them, and to break to the plow a drove of half-grown mules and horse colts that were on the place. By this means probably half of the farm could be plowed and cultivated. Simon told each man that under the changed order of things it was "every fellow for himself, even if the devil got the hindmost." It was only a question of a short time now when the Confederacy would collapse, as Johnson was fleeing before

Sherman in the Carolinas, and Lee, having evacuated Richmond, was hard pressed by Grant. Every State had been invaded, and in a few weeks the Confederate Government would fall to pieces and the soldiers return home, Colonel R. among the number, and he could then take charge of the plantation himself and make any change he saw fit.

Simon was satisfied, however, that this dividing up of the hands in squads would meet with the approbation of Colonel R., who would probably be a month later coming home than the other soldiers, as he was in prison in the far North when the Southern armies surrendered.

Before going to work under the new regime Simon made a visit to Colonel R.'s cotton and found it all O.K. He and Elsie then went to battle against "General Green," who had begun his depredations on the growing crop by this temporary cessation of hostilities against him. The crop was half made when Colonel R. made his appearance on his place. He expressed himself as well pleased in the way each hand was making use of what facilities the military cyclone had left in its path, and for them to carry things on as they were then doing, and when the crop was gathered he would give them a liberal share of it. The harvest proved to be a bountiful one, and the negroes were greatly elated at the success of this their first attempt to farm without an overseer or foreman. Colonel R. had a private interview with Simon, when both went to inspect the cotton that Simon had been intrusted with. They found it intact and in a good state of preservation. Simon then and there made a full confession of his share in the attempted escape of Elsie and child, of his apprehension and imprisonment, of his letter to him and its return, of his letter to his mistress advising her of the gold, and that it would be best to move it, etc.

The Colonel replied that he would have liberated Elsie and the child anyway, and didn't much blame him in trying to effect their escape, and that the only blame he attached to it was the sending off with the party Jack and Jim. However, he was satisfied with Simon's stewardship, and would now proceed to count him out the ten thousand dollars in gold which he had promised him, and that he would engage him as superintendent on his farm for the ensuing year at a salary of two thousand dollars per annum, thus literally carrying out their compact. It is needless to say that Simon hired a substitute to plow the oxen.

They returned to the farm, had all the ex-slaves assembled, when the Colonel made them a nice, short speech, commending them for their faithfulness during his absence in the army; that the Confederacy had been beaten, the war was over, and that they were free men, women and children; that whosoever may have been responsible for slavery in the United States, that whether it was right or wrong, the South had resorted to the arbitrament of arms, and as a result they were free, and that next year he would contract with any or all who wanted to farm on his place, under the super-intendency of Simon. During this talk he had gotten a good look at Octavia, not knowing whose child it was, called Simon aside, and asked whose it was; that it was a beautiful child, and looked as if it were pure white. Simon then said that it was a delicate subject, but that as he had asked for information, he would give it to him. The child was Elsie's, and she says that he, the Colonel, is its father. He then admitted to Simon that it was so, and that, while at home on furlough at one time during the war, he so far transgressed the laws of virtue, as to have an innocent, illegitimate child brought into existence. He also said that Elsie was not so much to blame as he, and that he was ashamed of his conduct, all of which was in the past, and could not be undone, and that he would atone, as far as possible, for his transgression, give Octavia the best education, in every branch, that time, money and labor would procure, and that, at his death, he would remember Octavia in his will, all of which was scrupulously carried out. The only conditions imposed were that the child be given to Simon, who would be her trustee or agent, in carrying all these things out, which had to be done secretly.

CHAPTER VIII

COTTON PROWLING— EMPLOYING OCTAVIA'S GOVERNESS.

Not long after the Southern soldiers came home, they began a wholesale prowling of government cotton, and in some instances, private cotton was stolen. The status of this government cotton was as follows: The Confederate government issued bonds, with a liberal rate of interest, exchanging them with the planters for their cotton, and in this way, a large amount had been acquired, half of which probably was still in warehouses and gin houses throughout the Southern States. Of course, this property, on the collapse of the Confederacy, by all moral and legal right, became the property of the United States government.

When the soldiers came home, they were without money, clothes, and in many instances, without anything to eat, especially if their homes were in the path of either army.

They claimed that they were violating no law of God or man

in taking this cotton. However, the pulpits in the country came out strongly against this practice, saying that if it was wrong to take private cotton, it was as much so to take public cotton; that the latter was nothing more nor less than wholesale theft. By some means, the whereabouts of Colonel R.'s cotton was found out, and it was whispered around, that it was government cotton. I would say here that Colonel R. had made a liberal donation of cotton to his government for bonds, but that every bale had been delivered and carried off. A raid was projected on this cotton on a certain night, but when they got there they found it guarded, Colonel R. and Simon having slept there since this cotton-prowling began. The leader of the raid claimed that it was government cotton, and that the raiders were going to have it. Colonel R. protested that it was not government cotton, but his own private property, and that if they got it they would have to do so over his dead body, and that he had help and was well armed. The night was dark, and fearing that it might be well guarded, and not knowing how many they had to oppose, the raiders decided that "discretion was the better part of valor," and left without molesting the cotton.

Colonel R. immediately hired every wagon and team, hauled the cotton to the river, shipped it to New Orleans by the first boat, and realized fifty cents per pound in gold for it, and as there were about one thousand bales, the reader can calculate, at five hundred pounds per bale, what a nice fortune the Colonel had, all of which had much to do with Octavia's future career.

While to all appearances Octavia was as white as the whitest, she had African blood coursing through her veins, which would debar her from Southern society. Social laws on this point were as rigid and unchangeable as the laws of the Medes and Persians.

Octavia was now about five years of age, most too young

to begin school, but the Colonel determined at once to hire a governess for her. Consequently he advertised in one of the foremost Northern dailies for one. He was not long in receiving answers to his "ad." One reply, from the interior of New York State, pleased him more than any of the others, the lady giving as reference one of his former colleagues in Congress. Several letters passed between the two, he telling her that if she accepted she would have to teach the niece of his ex-slave foreman, both of whom, however, were more white than black, and would pass as white where they were not known. By teaching in this family she would be socially ostracized by the white people of the country, and that hers would be a life of seclusion. But if she would accept and make the sacrifice he would make the liberal offer of fifteen hundred dollars per annum, she and Octavia to spend three months anywhere North in each year, the governess to teach her the nine scholastic months at Octavia's home. The Colonel gave her a description of Octavia, telling her that she would have an exceptionally bright and beautiful child to teach. Her board in Simon's family would cost her nothing, and all her hotel and traveling expenses would be paid by Colonel R. during each vacation, this contract to hold good as long as both parties were satisfied. The lady hesitated quite awhile, thinking it would be too great a sacrifice to be socially ostracized by her own race. But this was such an exceptionally good offer, and as she could break the contract after the first nine months, if she wished, she wrote Colonel R. a letter of acceptance. She at once made preparations to leave and was soon on her way South. She found a nice family and a most interesting child. We will have a good deal to do with the governess, and will call her Miss Mildred. She began her duties at once, and of course all of Octavia's studies were primary. Governess and pupil at once fell in love with each other, which ripened as the years went by. It was clearly a case of love at first sight. Octavia proved to be an apt scholar, and was soon ready to go in a higher grade. It was wonderful with what avidity one so young could grasp, comprehend and commit the lessons given her by Miss Mildred.

The governess was making splendid progress with her charge, when there was an occurrence which came near causing her to throw up her contract and return North.

At this time there were in the Southern States what was known as the "Ku-Klux-Klan," a secret organization, somewhat similar probably to the "White Caps." They could have been called "white" also, as they always had on a mask and long white gown, their horses also being covered with the same material to escape detection.

This order raided towns and certain sections of the country at night, but no one ever heard of any damage being done by them except what will now be related: One dark night there came to Simon's home probably twenty of these hideous-looking creatures, and called Simon out and demanded Octavia of him. He wanted to know why, when the leader of these ghosts told him that Mrs. ——, living in the town of ——, fifteen miles away, had had her little five-year-old girl Octavia stolen from her, and must have it; that the present laws of the country were inadequate to protect the people, and that the "Ku-Klux-Klan" was a law and order league, and attended to all cases such as child stealing, wife beaters, hog thieves, etc., and that he, Simon, nor his family, would not be molested unless they resisted their taking Octavia. Half a dozen of them dismounted and went into the house, almost frightening the women and Octavia out of their lives. They took Octavia out of the house amid the screams of Elsie and Miss Mildred. Simon was detained outside at the point of a pistol. They mounted, one taking Octavia in front of him, telling her she could return on the morrow if she was not the right child. They went off in full gallop and were soon out of sight. Simon heard them tell his niece that she could return on the morrow if she was not the right one. He went in to tell his sister of this and then to get his horse, which he had recently bought, to follow them. He found Elsie in a convulsion and Miss Mildred so wrought up with fright that she was not far from it. Consequently it was out of the question to leave them. He could get no one else there, every negro being as badly frightened, at the strange, weird sight they had seen that night. Wishing, hoping, praying that no harm would befall Octavia, he set about to do what he could for the grief-stricken and frightened governess and his unconscious sister. By repeated assurances to Miss Mildred that all would be well with Octavia, he in a great measure got her quieted. They then went to work on Elsie, who was unconscious and of course not able to talk. They worked with her the night through, and as the sun was rising she regained consciousness, and Simon was endeavoring to assure her of the safety of Octavia, telling what he heard the leader of the gang tell her, and that he would get his horse and leave immediately and go for Octavia, when there was a knock at the door, and on opening it there stood Octavia, who ran into her mother's arms and was caressed and kissed again and again by all. Of course their joy and happiness knew no bounds, especially Elsie, who began alternately to cry and laugh and couldn't stop. This alarmed them as they did not know what to do. Octavia had returned, and it seemed that last night's experience with her would be repeated. However, it soon wore off, and she was well of the hysterics. "Weeping may endure for a night, but joy cometh in the morning." We will let the negro who brought Octavia make explanation in his own way.

Said he to Simon: "Ole Miss axed me to bring dis purty little gal back to yu. She is bery sorry, 'deed, dat dem 'jutty Klux' fetched yu little gal tu her; dat she look like her gal sum, but she ain't de wun. She say akcept her 'poligies, an' she hope Mr. Simon won't tink ennyways hard ob her." Simon thanked the negro for bringing Octavia back, and asked him to tell his "Ole Miss" that he didn't blame her in any way, at the same time putting a ten-dollar gold piece in the negro's hands. The negro bowed and scraped all over the yard and bade them adieu.

It leaked out that Henry, Simon's quondam enemy, told some of the clan that Simon and his sister had a white girl named Octavia which they had stolen from Mrs. —— at ——. This lady's stolen daughter was named Octavia, and the Ku-Klux took it for granted that this was the stolen child. Henry had told a half truth—the girl at Simon's was named Octavia and was about five years old, but that she was Mrs. ——'s child was a willful lie, and he knew it. A half truth is as bad as a whole lie. Simon threatened vengeance against him. Simon wanted to prosecute the mob, but could get no evidence as to who a single member was.

CHAPTER IX.

PROGRESS IN STUDIES.

After this experience Miss Mildred told Simon that she could not live in any such a country, and that she would have to throw up her contract and go back North. She said that with a little forethought she might have known this, as everything was unsettled after such a war that had been ended but a few months. She had no objection to a single member of his family, and she had a high regard for him, and really loved Elsie and Octavia.

He then asked her to reconsider the matter, as he would move to the city of M., then and since a flourishing town. There they could have police protection, which was not available in the country. She said she would think over the matter and decide in a day or so. Simon immediately wrote to Colonel R. that he would have to throw up his contract as superintendent, telling him the reason why. The Colonel replied that he was loath to give him up, but under the circumstances he would have to do so.

After getting the Colonel's letter Miss Mildred agreed to remain if there was an immediate removal. Simon said all the time he asked was to go to the city and buy a house and lot, which he did, and the family was soon installed in their new home.

Simon now put the gold which Colonel R. had given him for his faithfulness to good use. He, in addition to his dwelling, bought a storehouse on one of the principal business streets, and put a large stock of goods in it. He proved to be as successful a merchant as he was a farmer. He was soon doing a large business, having to employ a bookkeeper and a large number of clerks.

Soon after Simon left Colonel R. had a good opportunity to sell his plantation to good advantage, which he did, getting cash for it.

This, with his cotton money, made a handsome fortune, which he judiciously invested in stocks, bonds, etc.

In his new home Simon prospered, and knew that here he would have protection when the shades of night drew her curtain around them.

Octavia's life from now on was what would be incident to the life of any school-girl under a governess from six years old until sixteen, when she graduated. She had no hairbreadth escapes as in the past. She advanced rapidly in her studies, Miss Mildred having no trouble at all with her. She always recited perfect lessons—in a word, was as near perfect as mortal could be. She accompanied Miss Mildred North on her vacation trips, which were generally spent at Saratoga Springs. Octavia always had a bountiful supply of money, which her uncle gave her, and consequently wanted for nothing. It is well to say here that a check from Colonel R. was always on hand for such purposes.

When Octavia was eight years old Colonel R. sent her an eight-hundred-dollar piano. At ten years of age he sent the following fine instruments: Organ, guitar, violin and harp, together with a good supply of art material. He was simply fulfilling his purpose to give her a finished education, and no girl was considered "finished" who was not well grounded in music and art. Octavia thought her uncle was giving her all these musical instruments and art material. She never knew until in after years who was the real donor. Simon was indeed a faithful agent and trustee.

Miss Mildred had been Octavia's governess for seven or eight years, when one bright morning, just before her and Octavia's annual vacation, she was dumfounded to receive a proposal of marriage from Simon. During all these years Cupid had been shooting darts into his heart; he had been a silent lover of Miss Mildred. Time and again it was on the point of his tongue to make this declaration, but knowing that he was of an inferior race, and Miss Mildred far his superior, he shrank from it. During all this time Miss Mildred never suspected the sentiments he had for her, and never dreamed that he had any other than a high regard for her as a faithful teacher to his beautiful niece. She kindly refused him, telling him that she was too much in love with Octavia and engrossed in teaching her to love anybody else. There were stringent laws in this State against miscegenation, and his proposal to elope was out of the question, as, if she ever married, that was one way she wanted to avoid. She said she had a high regard for him as a man of honor and integrity, and trusted that this refusal would not mar their friendship. She said she was wrapped up in his niece, who had a bright future before her, and while only one more session remained before she would enter college, she would regret having to part with her; that she had had a pleasant home in his family, and would return after vacation to put in as faithful service in finishing up Octavia for college as it was in her power to give. This skillful and adroit changing of the subject relieved the embarrassment to both, and the interview ended by Simon wishing for her and Octavia a pleasant vacation at Saratoga.

Simon afterwards said that if he could not marry one of a superior he would not marry one of an inferior race.

In this connection I would say that it is one of the leading characteristics of the negro to want to marry one of better blood, with straight hair and white skin. Consequently mulattoes and quadroons are in demand. Especially do they bank on straight hair; if he or she have straight hair it hides all the ugliness of the face. It is a common remark that females of the white race resort to all kinds of ways to make their hair kinky or frizzly, while those of the negro race would give an empire for straight hair.

Again, the negro suitor makes no objection because one has gone astray, and has one or more illegitimate children. If she has straight hair and a bright skin, it makes no difference about any of her past indiscretions.

While on the subject of matrimony among negroes, I would say that they don't consider it a violation of the laws of God to have a plurality of wives. True, they have one legal wife, but at the same time they have one or more secret or illegal wives. This is the rule, and prevails among their leading men in the churches—stewards, deacons, trustees, Sunday-school superintendents, etc. A great deal is said against Mormonism and polygamy, which some one has termed a "twin evil of slavery." There is no doubt that Mormonism is one of the foulest blots upon the escutcheon of the United States. It is passing strange that such a curse could find a lodgment in "the best government the world ever saw." It is not strange as to slavery, because that was recognized in the Constitution.

I would make the point that there is just as much polygamy among the negroes as there is in Utah, and to be consistent the authorities should cry out against one as the other. But it may be said that it is the States' business to regulate this thing. If so, let them do it. "Consistency, thou art a jewel."

CHAPTER X.

READY FOR COLLEGE.

Octavia was now fourteen, and with her governess was spending their vacation North. While they were absent Brutus came to the city and gave himself up to the sheriff for the murder of Cæsar about eighteen years before. On a preliminary trial he easily proved that he did it in self-defense and was discharged. He immediately applied to Simon for employment. Simon was in need of some one to work his garden, chop wood and do the chores on the place, and as Brutus was a good worker, and for the sake of old times, he employed him. Brutus doubtless had a motive in this, as he had not been there long before he proposed to Elsie. She indignantly repelled him, telling him that she did not want him or any other "kinky-headed" negro. Brutus thought that, as Elsie had at one time in her life wandered from the paths of rectitude, she would readily consent to a marriage. But in this "he reckoned without his host." He continued, however, in Simon's employ and made a good servant. During the whole time that Simon had been a resident of the city he and his household had been very exclusive, holding aloof from the large negro population of that place. Notwithstanding this exclusiveness, Octavia and her governess were not unknown, and more than one young man of Caucasian blood made efforts to get an introduction to Octavia, but in vain. They had found out that Octavia was one-eighth African, but that made no difference, one or two declaring that she was so lovely and accomplished that if necessary they would make a "Gretna Green" affair of it.

There were so many favorable comments on Octavia's beauty when she appeared on the streets that Miss Mildred thought best for her not to be seen so often, and made their visits less frequent. The summer vacation soon sped away, and teacher and pupil were at their posts of duty to put in their last session together. Miss Mildred said it was a pleasure to teach such an apt scholar, and Octavia declared that it was an equal pleasure to be taught by such a proficient and competent teacher.

The affection that existed between the two was wonderful, something on the order of the love that David and Jonathan had for each other. Time did not drag heavily on teacher and pupil, as it does in some schools. The session came to an end and the time at hand when there would have to be a separation. It was decided, however, that Octavia should spend the summer North with her teacher, thus postponing the time of separation three months. Miss Mildred's work with Octavia was done. She would now turn her over to higher educators. Ten years before she took hold, as it were, of the budding mind of Octavia. She saw it gradually grow and unfold, and ere long she would be a full-grown, intellectual flower. She had faithfully performed her part in imparting instruction, and Octavia had equally performed hers in receiving it. The sad day arrived when Miss Mildred had to part with Simon and Elsie—she to return to her far away Northern home and they to remain "away down South in Dixie."

The fact that teacher and pupil had to separate in three months marred the otherwise pleasant vacation which they would have enjoyed together. It was more of a perfunctory sojourn together, both dreading the day of separation.

Simon consulted Colonel R. as to the college Octavia should attend, and it was left to Miss Mildred, who recommended the large female seminary at ——, Massachusetts. Colonel R. then wrote the President of this seminary that he had a ward, a young lady of rare beauty and intellect, whom he desired to enter the ensuing session, and that in addition to his regular fees he would pay for any extra work done for his ward liberally, and for him to spare neither time, labor nor money to advance this young lady, that he wanted for her the best that the institution afforded. He informed the President that she could finish in two sessions, and that she would be present at the beginning of the coming session.

Three months soon sped away, and Octavia and her ex-teacher must part. Their feelings can be better imagined than described. It had to be witnessed to form a correct idea of the bond that existed. Miss Mildred accompanied Octavia to the train and both were entwined in each other's arms, kissing and caressing, and would separate, and Octavia start for the train, when she would return, and the same performance be repeated, and repeated again, until the conductor shouted "All aboard," and the train moved off, bearing a desolate heart, and leaving one equally so at the station.

Octavia was going to a large city, an entire stranger. How desolate one feels in a large city, with acres of humanity around you and not acquainted with a single person! Reader, you will have to realize this to get its full meaning. Miss Mildred had sent a telegram to the President to meet the young lady from the South on the arrival of the train. He did so, and endeavored to make it as pleasant as possible for her, knowing she was a perfect stranger and far from home. The school began the next day, and being engrossed in her studies Octavia soon forgot her loneliness. It was not long before she was a favorite with teachers and pupils. With such a being it could not be otherwise. She was always referred to as "the lovely young lady from the South." She matriculated simply as "Octavia," and when the President insisted that she write her full name (in reality she had none), she would reply "that will do."

This was a strange condition to be in—a lovely, intelligent young lady without a name! Whether the President thought anything strange about this peculiarity was never known. In college, as with her governess, she made rapid strides in all her studies, excelling in elocution, music and art.

She captivated the musical director almost on sight. He knew, however, that propriety forbade his making it known to her. At every musical recital every eye was focussed on her. She received the plaudits and commendation of teacher and pupils. The following appeared in one of the leading dailies of that city in regard to one of her recitals: "The recital yesterday eve at the —— Seminary was indeed a musical treat to the large and cultured audience who graced the occasion. Miss Octavia, a beautiful and accomplished young lady from Alabama, rendered several difficult pieces on the piano which were grand. To have heard these strains one would have thought he or she was listening to Rubenstein, Mozart or others of the masters. It was a greater treat to hear her sing. That voice! It reminded you of Adelina Patti, Jenny Lind or other famous prima donnas. Musical Director ——, of the seminary, is to be congratulated in having such a talented young lady to teach. He also deserves the thanks of the public for getting up such a musical treat."

The above notice is only one of similar import that appeared at different times in the various city papers while Octavia was at the seminary. The session progressed apace; the musical director all the while becoming more and more infatuated with his Southern magnolia, as he termed her. The session at last came to a close, much to the regret of the musical director. Octavia's success had been phenomenal from the first. Her music teacher, being so infatuated, was probably partial, and gave her extra attention. While it was Colonel R.'s wish that she receive extra attention, for which teachers would get extra pay, this teacher of music imparted this extra instruction because of his extra love which he had for his fair pupil from the South. He had always boasted that he could withstand the charms of the loveliest, but he had at last been conquered and had surrendered, "horse, foot and dragoons," to the loveliest being that he had ever beheld. He resolved to make an effort to make her his bride. Consequently he indited the following epistle, which he decided to send her on the evening of commencement, this being grand concert night, and the closing of the school:

"Dear Miss Octavia: I suppose you will be surprised to receive such a note from me, but I don't see why, as my every look and act for the past nine months plainly indicated that I was passionately, devotedly and blindly in love with you. But the rules of the seminary as well as propriety forbade that I should tell you so. The session having closed I now say so, with all the emphasis of my soul, that you are the loveliest and most intelligent girl that these heretofore woman-resisting eyes have ever beheld. Have the breezes wafted this magnolia from the South to make me happy or miserable the balance of my days? Heaven grant that it may be the former. I have surrendered to the most attractive object in existence. This conquest was made innocently on your part, you not having the remotest idea that I entertained any such feelings for you. You are the essence of quintessence; the nectar that Jupiter sipped of the gods was not half so sweet. But enough until I see you and have a personal interview, which I hope you will grant immediately. I anxiously await until the messenger returns. Yours, madly in love with the beautiful flower from Alabama,

"Your Music Teacher."

Upon reading this passionate effusion she burst into tears, and it was quite awhile before she was calm enough to send the following note:

"My Efficient Music Teacher: Your note has just been received and contents regretfully noted. I am pained to have such sentiments from you, and sorry that I have innocently caused such. Were I ever so willing to reciprocate the sentiments expressed, there is an impassable barrier between us, the cause of which I cannot and will not explain. I am sure this is only a passing fancy with you, and on reflection you will soon forget me, and 'Richard will be himself again.' I leave in the early morning for my home in Dixie, where I can have the pleasure of again being with my dear mother and uncle. I appreciate your extra efforts in my behalf in my music lessons, but I cannot and will not grant the interview. Your music pupil from Alabama,

"Octavia."

Upon reading this respectful but positive refusal he tore it in fragments and tossed it out of the window. He then wrote the following note to President ——, of the seminary:

"Dear Sir: Please engage the services of Miss ——, who has been my proficient assistant during the session just closed, as your musical directress during the ensuing session. Don't ask me to explain. Yours truly, ——."

After writing this he deliberately took his pistol, and placing it to his forehead, fired. The occupants of the house, hearing the report, rushed into his room and found him on the floor, pistol by his side and bullet hole in his forehead, from which blood was trickling. They soon discovered the note to President ——, of the seminary, sent it to him, with instructions to come at once and bring a surgeon with him. The two were soon there, and the surgeon, on examining, found that the would-be suicide failed to make a center shot, the ball being deflected and going around the skull, where he extracted it without much trouble. He soon regained consciousness from the concussion, arranged his affairs and left on an early train, never to return. There were glowing accounts in the morning papers of the grand concert, complimenting the director; also giving glowing descriptions of Octavia's singing and playing, and in the same issue giving a detailed account of the tragedy at No. —— —— Street, when the musical director shot and thought he had killed himself. As a natural consequence the city, early the next morning, was all agog about the "Grand Concert" and the attempted suicide of the musical director who so successfully conducted it. Everybody was amazed, as no clew could be found for his deed and flight. Octavia called at the President's house on her way to the train to bid him farewell. She inquired of him the cause of the commotion in the city. He told her he was surprised to find that she had not heard of the attempted suicide of his musical director, and her music teacher the past session. He told her of his note requesting him to employ the assistant directress as principal the ensuing session, which he would have to do, as the director had fled and no cause could be found for all this, as he had left in good shape, at least as to money matters. She could easily have told him the cause, but kept her counsel. It was with difficulty that she could restrain her tears while he was telling this.

The President congratulated her on the success she had attained in the seminary, and told of the encomiums he had heard heaped upon her, and after giving her a pressing invitation to return and graduate at the seminary, he bade her an affectionate farewell. She was soon aboard the Pullman sleeper and on her way to the Southland. Being an entire stranger to every one on the train she had opportunity to read the account in one of the city papers, which she had purchased, of the preceding night's events. She was not a vain or egotistical girl, and the papers' compliments of herself did not "turn her head." She was only gratified that she really merited these plaudits. She was grieved, however, to know that she was the innocent cause of the attempted suicide of the musical director, and of President —— being deprived of his efficient services the ensuing term. The lightning speed of the train soon landed her in her mother's arms, who, with Simon, gave her a joyous welcome. She had much to say to them of her seminary life, of the plaudits of the press and people and the farewell commendation of the President, and when she told them of the attempted suicide of her music teacher, and she being the cause, she broke down and wept bitterly. They comforted her by telling her that her next music teacher would be a lady, and surely that could not happen again.

She whiled away the hours of vacation at her piano or organ or with her guitar, violin or harp. Several attempts to gain admission to her society by some of the best white bloods of the city were made, but all in vain. She always refused, telling them that she was a school-girl striving for an education, and she would admit nothing that would detract her from her studies.

Three months soon rolled away, and she bade her mother and uncle farewell, she hoped for the last time, they showering upon her many God bless you's and best wishes.

The second and last session of her seminary life was but a repetition of the first, minus the musical director, and another variation, which will soon be narrated.

Let us now return for awhile to Octavia's home and notice an event that was destined to have an important bearing upon Octavia's post graduate life. A wealthy lady from the North came to the city with a letter of introduction from Miss Mildred to Simon. She was simply making a tour of the South, and Miss Mildred knowing that her friend would be in the city where she had spent ten years of her life, gave her this letter. Anything emanating from Miss Mildred was all right, in Simon's and his sister's estimation, and they gave the lady a cordial welcome, bidding her spend her time with them. She respectfully declined, but said that she would come around often while in the city. This lady had a costly diamond ring, valued at one thousand dollars, which she had taken from her finger one day while at Simon's residence. While in the sitting-room she had carelessly laid the ring on the dresser and forgot it until some time afterwards, when she could find it nowhere. All of the occupants of the house were questioned about it; search for it was made, but it could be found nowhere. It was clearly a case of theft. But who did it? was the question. Surely Miss Mildred would not give her a letter of introduction to a family any one of whom would steal a ring laid on a dresser. Yet she had lost it in their house, and as Simon was at his place of business suspicion at once pointed to Elsie as the thief. The lady put the case in a detective's hands to ferret out. Simon had a next door neighbor, a negro woman as black as the proverbial ace of spades, whom he had spotted as the real thief.

She was frequently employed to do scouring and cleaning up in his house, and while she was not doing any work of that kind on the day the ring was stolen, she could easily have stealthily gone into the sitting-room and got it. This woman told several parties that she saw Elsie have a fine diamond ring. The detective found this out and questioned the woman, who confirmed the report. The detective at once suspicioned the woman and also that the woman said she would swear that she saw Elsie have on a fine diamond ring.

Simon at once employed a rising young attorney to defend his sister, as he knew she would be arraigned in court. The Grand Jury was in session, Elsie was indicted, and the trial set for Monday of the next week. The trial came off, and there was a hotly contested legal battle between the opposing counsel, Elsie's lawyer making a fine speech in her behalf and having no trouble in impeaching the evidence of the only witness the State had. Elsie's lawyer proved and brought out the fact that this woman, the State's witness, was in love with Brutus and Brutus in love with Elsie, and that she would swear to Elsie having a diamond ring, when, as the woman thought, Elsie would be convicted, sent to State's prison, and she would have no opposition to Brutus' heart and hand. The attorney made the telling point, that "green eyed jealousy" was why this woman had perjured herself. The jury gave Elsie a unanimous acquittal. This woman, the State's only witness, was then arrested for perjury, when she confessed to having stolen the ring, and to swearing to a lie on Elsie, and handed the ring to the presiding judge. This woman was "hoisted on her own petard," being sent to the penitentiary, instead of Elsie.

Simon thought best to keep all this from Octavia, to whom we will now return. There were two lawyers in the city where Octavia was attending school, who had been struck, the previous session, with Octavia's beauty and accomplishments, but had kept it to themselves. During this session, they attended every recital at the seminary, and the church that Octavia attended. They could, at least, admire at a distance. There were stringent rules, in the seminary, forbidding the girls from having gentlemen visitors. To this, Octavia made no objection, as was done by many other students. It is needless to say that the admiration of these lawyers increased, as the session wore on, Octavia being ignorant of anything of the kind. These men, by some means, found out that the other was in love with this young lady from Alabama, and became bitter enemies, because of this. The session closed, and Octavia graduated with the highest honors, taking all of the prizes, some of which were valuable.

The city papers were again highly complimentary of Octavia, and predicted a brilliant career, for "the accomplished young lady from Alabama." The President of the seminary agreed that on the night of the grand concert, the girls would be allowed to receive attentions from the young men, if agreeable. Octavia's silent rivals met up with each other, on their way to the concert, when the subject of the girls being allowed that night to receive gentlemen attendants, was broached. One claimed the privilege of seeing Miss Octavia; the other said he would enjoy that privilege himself, both showing how egotistical they were. Miss Octavia's feelings were not taken into consideration. They kept contending, until a difficulty ensued, both pulling their pistols and firing at the same time, both falling, one dead and the other wounded. Of course the police were soon there, and the wounded man gave the facts which have just been related.

The concert came off, and Octavia carried off the laurels of the evening. She might not have done so, however, if she had been told that two men, perfect strangers to her had fought a duel about her, one getting killed, and the other wounded. "Where ignorance is bliss, 'tis folly to be wise." After the conclusion of the concert, all this was told her, when she immediately went to her room, and was weeping, when the President of the seminary knocked, and was admitted. He inquired the cause of her grief when she said that again she was the innocent cause of another tragedy; one man dead and another wounded, on her account. The President then tried to comfort her, telling her that he was more the cause of it than any one; that he had removed the restrictions that night, and that these men, not knowing that she would see either one, got into a quarrel as to which one should see her, with the results as stated.

He then complimented her on her attainments and brilliant success in the seminary; of her original graduating essay, etc., and assured her that she would always find a fast friend in him, and wished her unbounded success in life, and would now sadly say farewell. When he was gone, she again was convulsed with tears; bitter tears, at parting with her presiding teacher, and of being innocently the cause of the tragedy that had just been enacted.

She retired weeping, and cried herself to sleep, and was awakened early the next morning by her hackman, to take her to the train, which was almost ready to start. She hastily dressed, and with her baggage was soon in the hack, arriving just in time for Octavia to board the moving train. She was bidding farewell to the city of her triumphs, in which two tragedies had been enacted on her account, and was on her way to her own Southern, sunny, happy home, at the same time wondering what would be her future.

CHAPTER XI.

IN THE RED CROSS SERVICE.

In this age of the world, distance is no object, and Octavia was soon in the bosom of her family, and would follow that career, which God in His Providence would work out for her.

Simon and Elsie were proud of Octavia, as they had a right to be. She had just graduated with highest honors from one of the foremost Northern seminaries, and had brought home a lot of prizes, some of them valuable.

She was beautiful and didn't know it; accomplished, without ostentation; and was modest, gentle, courteous and dignified.

Brutus, who was still in Simon's employ as servant, and kept in a servant's place, frequently said, that if he didn't know to the contrary, he would say that Octavia, "wuz a sho' nuff white 'oman."

Of course she had to tell her uncle and mother about the lawyers fighting a duel about her; of one getting killed, and the other wounded; and she the innocent cause. Simon consoled her with the fact that she was at home now, and could seclude herself, if she so desired, and not be molested by men. She said she could not live the life of a hermit, regardless of what the men thought of her.

They then told her of the diamond ring occurrence, and that they had purposely kept it from her while at school, and determined to await her return, when they could explain the matter better, orally.

Not long after her return, she was in Simon's store, and Elsie's attorney happened to come in. Simon, in an humble, courteous way introduced his niece to the attorney, as "Octavia," who had just graduated with distinguished honors, from the foremost seminary in the North. Both acknowledged the introduction with a bow, after which, Octavia left the store, and the attorney, after making some purchases, doing the same. That was a brief meeting, but Cupid had put in his work. The attorney on his way home determined, if he could, to know more of this lovely being. It must be said here, that the attorney had heard of her beauty and accomplishments, and of her lowly birth, and having one-eighth African blood coursing through her veins. The next day he was in Simon's store again, and remarked that he would like to hear his niece play and sing, and to examine her art collection. Simon said he would be pleased to have him do so, and thought that his niece would make no objection. He said he would be around after tea to enjoy this pleasure. Will wonders never cease? Here was one of the leading attorneys of the city, and purest of the pure Caucasians, becoming smitten with an octoroon. Simon then reminded him of the social barriers that existed and of the effect it might have on his practice, and on him socially. He left the store, remarking "Society be d——." At supper, Simon told his niece that the attorney would be there to hear her play and sing, and to inspect her art collection. She said that it must not be a social call. Simon went back to his store, thinking a lot, but saying nothing. He had been in public business so long, that he could read human character almost like a book. He was satisfied in his mind that Elsie's attorney had succumbed to Octavia's charms, and he would await developments with anxiety.

This attorney was young and handsome and already had gained a lucrative practice at the bar, and was still adding fame to his laurels. Notwithstanding her short acquaintance, Octavia confessed secretly that she was favorably impressed with him, but at the same time, she knew that social barriers would prevent his paying her and she receiving his attentions.

At the appointed time, he was ringing the bell for admittance, which was answered by Elsie, who invited him into the parlor.

Octavia soon came in, when he told her that he had come to have the pleasure of hearing her play and sing, and to inspect her art collection. She gave him a cordial greeting, saying that he flattered her, but, that if she had any talent for music and art, he was welcome to witness and hear the same. He expressed himself as delighted with her paintings; and then requested her to play and sing. She rendered her graduating recital in music, on the piano. He thought it grand and magnificent, and requested her to sing, which she did, using the organ first, and then, guitar, as an accompaniment.

He was charmed, and said that he had never heard her equal. That her voice was sweet, but not inaudible; melodious, but not husky; loud, but not boisterous; clear and harmonious; and that but few prima donnas, who were delighting thousands, by their voices on the stage, came up to her standard of singing.

On leaving, he asked the pleasure of again calling, that he had often heard of her, but had not had the pleasure of meeting her until their brief introduction the day before at her uncle's store—but, that now, he had come, seen and heard, and was conquered.

He said that like the "Queen of Sheba," he could also say, that "the half had not been told." She politely replied that the proprieties of Southern social life would not permit a social call from him on her, but that if it was any pleasure, he might come and hear her play and sing, and to inspect her paintings—he might do so, but not in a social way. He thanked her, and left, and on his way home, hurled anathemas against social laws, so far as they separated him and Octavia. Of course, he knew it would not do for the races to intermingle and commingle, indiscriminately. But Octavia was so near pure white, that it amounted to "a distinction without a difference." That he was passionately in love with Octavia there was no doubt. What must he do? What would the effect of these visits, if known, have on his practice?

He was not wholly indifferent to public opinion, and while he knew what the opinion would be, he was determined to hear Octavia play and sing, let the consequences be what they may.

The attorney was not the only Caucasian who had succumbed to Octavia's charms. A wealthy real estate agent, and president of the local bank, was in the same predicament. He had repeatedly sought an introduction, but had never been able to reach the goal of his desires.

The attorney saw Simon, and asked him to say to his niece that he would come at 8 P.M., to hear some more of her singing. Simon did so. Whereat, she was pleased as well as sad. She cared more for the attorney than she was willing to admit. At the same time she knew that it was wrong, socially, for a white man to be making visits to her uncle's house. The public might think that his visits were purely on business, as he had been her mother's successful attorney. But, if they continued, their object would soon be found out. "You may fool all the people awhile, but you can't fool some of the people all the while." When the attorney came, she had on her "best bib and tucker," and never looked lovelier. Whether she wanted to make an additional impression, or not, on the attorney, the fact is she did. He came, saw and heard again, and was charmed and chained to the spot by her loveliness. He had often heard of Eden—he had found it. He did not see how there could be a more attractive paradise elsewhere. If allowed, he would remain—he was not like Mahomet, who, it is said, after a long hot day's journey over the desert sands, came in sight (just as the sun, as it were, was going down into the Mediterranean) of Damascus, surrounded by a desert and situated on those beautiful rivers, Pharpar and Abana,—Damascus, in which were bubbling fountains, gardens of olives, dates, figs, oranges and all manner of tropical fruits; streets shaded by royal palms, dotted here and there, with magnificent mosques with their lofty minarets, and lovely dwellings. This, after his weary, hot day's journey, was a charming sight, an enchanting spectacle; how he longed to slake his thirst from those bubbling springs, and bathe in those cool fountains, and then rest under those royal palms, or appease his hunger, by eating of those tropical fruits. He was tempted to enter, but after gazing longingly, he said, "it was ordained for man to enter paradise but once," and turned around and retraced his journey. With the attorney, it was different; he had entered this paradise, and knew he had to leave, but how? He arose to do so, and before he was aware of it, he was on his knees before the fair Octavia. He declared his love with all the fervor and ardor of a Castilian, and asked her heart and hand in marriage. He had successfully pleaded the case of her mother, on a false charge; might he not be as

71

successful in pleading his case before her, who was judge, counsel and jury?—his charge was true, that he loved her, adored her, worshipped her. She listened patiently until he finished, and then bade him rise and be seated. Like a chained captive, he obeyed. She then in a cool, quiet, dignified manner told him that she entertained feelings for him that she did not for any other man, and which she supposed writers of romance would call love, but that he knew and she knew that there was a social chasm between them, that could not be bridged—that both knew that the laws of the State were very stringent against the races intermarrying, and that it was wrong for him to propose, or for her to accept. Being a lawyer, he pleaded that it might be a legal wrong, but that there was no moral wrong, and to get around this legal objection, they could soon go to a State that had no laws on the subject. She then told him of her humble birth—that of a slave—and of her life afterwards. He replied that he knew all, but that that did not have a feather's weight with him—that it was not birth, wealth or environment that made noble men or women; but that it was true worth and merit, modesty, beauty, accomplishments, gentleness and dignity, all of which she possessed to a most marked degree. She replied that she was created under the present environments and whether it was fortunate or unfortunate for her, she must submit to it, and that it would be wrong to question the wisdom or unwisdom as to how she was brought into existence. She then told the attorney that her future career would be one of mercy; that she thought it her duty to ameliorate as far as possible, the sufferings of mankind, and that she had decided before graduation, the Lord permitting, to join the Red Cross Society, and asked to be sent to Europe, for a position with the Russian Army, that was then waging war against Turkey. She hated to leave home—her mother, uncle—and as to friends, she had none.

The attorney protested that he was her friend, lover, and would be her husband, whenever she said the word. She insisted that it would be better for them to part; but, that when in a foreign land, she would if it afforded any pleasure, carry on a friendly correspondence with him. He thanked her, telling her that that would be one grain of comfort; but begged her to reconsider, and not bury herself, as it were, in nursing those despicable Cossacks and Turks.

She said her decision was unalterable. With this, he took his leave, fearing she might never return. He consoled himself with the thought that she loved him, and if she ever returned, he would still have hopes of winning her. "Hope springs eternal in the human breast." Once get a woman to love a man, and all obstacles will as a rule be overcome.

CHAPTER XII.

IN FOREIGN LANDS— STRATEGY—LOVE CONQUERS.

Octavia made known to her uncle and mother the attorney's passionate proposal and pleading—of her previous determination to go on a mission of mercy, joining the Red Cross Society. Both pleaded with her to give up her European trip, whatever she did with the attorney. But secretly they wanted Octavia to accept him. Both liked him. A firm friendship had been formed. He had successfully pleaded Elsie's case, and would be pleased to see the match. But Octavia was of age, and marrying was a personal matter, and every one must choose for herself.

She was firm in her decision to go, and they soon saw that further pleading was of no use. It was only a question of short time to make the necessary arrangements for her departure. Just before her departure Colonel R. died. Just previous to his sickness and death, he wrote Simon to come to see him, as he wanted to confer with him on some important business. Simon went, and the Colonel said to him, that he did not think he had long to live, and that in his will, he would bequeath Octavia fifty thousand dollars in gold, and for him, Simon, to act as her agent and trustee, until Octavia chose to make use of it. Simon was grateful on behalf of his niece for this liberal bequest. Colonel R. said that this would be the crowning act of atonement for his wrong in bringing Octavia into the world. He said he had sought forgiveness for this act, and that he felt that God, for Christ's sake, had pardoned him; not only for this, but other wrongs. He said to Simon that he had heard of Octavia's brilliant success in college, of the plaudits of her teachers, press and public. If Octavia, said he, went to Europe, it would be simply to get rid of her suitors; that hers was an anomalous condition. She would not wed beneath herself, and the laws of the country forbid her marrying a white man. He would now bid farewell to his ex-foreman, for the last time, wishing him unbounded success in life.

Colonel R.'s heirs contested the will, or that part bequeathing the gold to Octavia, and made strenuous efforts to have the courts set it aside. Simon again employed Elsie's ex-attorney to defend that clause in the will. There was a fierce legal battle, but the will as a whole was sustained, and Octavia was left independent.

Octavia now departed on her mission of mercy, Simon and Elsie believing that they would never see her again. She was bidding farewell to home, kindred,—to all that she held most dear. "Yes, my native land, I leave thee, far in foreign lands to dwell." After arriving in New York, she soon obtained passports for St. Petersburg, Russia, taking the first steamer, and ere long, would be

"Out on the ocean, all boundless we ride."

After arriving in St. Petersburg, she made known her mission to the authorities, who appointed a guard to escort her to the Russian Army, and she was soon administering comfort to the sick and wounded. She really proved to be an angel of mercy, as her beauty alone often brought hope to the despairing one.

About two months after she began work as an agent of the Red Cross, she received a telegram that her mother had died from smallpox. It is trouble enough to lose a parent and be at her bedside, but to be in a foreign land, with an army which is fighting another, with not a single friend or acquaintance to comfort you, is heart-rending. This was the severest grief of her life. But, being engrossed by her duties, her grief was tempered. It is said that "duty is the sublimest word in the English language." Certainly, it is the best cure for trouble, grief, disappointments, or any of the ills of life.

Soon after this, she received a long letter of condolence from her attorney lover, on the death of her mother. This was quite a comfort, and she redoubled her efforts to comfort the sick, wounded, distressed, dying soldiers around her. While engaged in her mission of mercy, she became acquainted with Count ———, a gallant colonel in the Russian Army. This count, like the American attorney, fell desperately in love with her, and made it known the first opportunity, asking her hand in marriage as soon as hostilities ceased. She repelled his offer, telling him that among the sick, dead and dying, was no place to be thinking about anything of that kind. The count took his defeat philosophically, saying to his friends that he would bide his time and renew his suit for the fair American angel of mercy, in "the sweet by-and-by."

Octavia found time to correspond with her uncle, and her attorney lover, telling each how she had become fond of her work, and that it was not as objectionable as one would think.

The war finally closed, and Octavia determined to return to America, and render comfort to the soldiers who were then fighting the Indians on the plains. She had caught a severe cold, while discharging her duties at the front, which resulted in pneumonia, and for days her physician despaired of her life. Finally, he announced that the crisis had passed, and that good nursing would soon bring her round all right, and wired this welcome news to Simon. It required a month or more to recuperate and gain strength. In that time, she saw from the American papers, that the Indian war had ceased. Consequently, she decided to remain in the Russian capital, whither she had gone after hostilities, a year or more. She had found trouble in rightly discharging her duties, because of her inability to speak the Russian language. Consequently, she determined to master that, and a half dozen or more of the principal languages of Europe, during her stay in St. Petersburg. The signs of the times pointed to another European war, and she would stand in need of one or more of the languages she was studying.

Count —— again renewed his suit with the fair Octavia, promising her title, wealth, ease and pleasure, and as he was closely related to the reigning family, she would have access to the pleasures of the Royal Court of Russia. To all of his pleadings she would say nay, telling him that she did not come to Europe hunting a husband with a title, and that she was disgusted with the snobbery displayed by some American girls in hunting for a husband with a title to his name. She said she was a plain girl from Republo-Democratic America, and came to render succor, aid and comfort to the sick, distressed, dead, wounded and dying, of the Russian Army, and that her mission to that particular field being ended, she was studying the various foreign languages, while waiting for another opportunity to continue her mission of mercy. This reply was characteristic of her. It is a fact that many American girls, disgust the public in their chase after titled husbands—they furnishing the wealth, and the husband, the empty title. Away with such snobbishness! Simon kept her supplied with what funds she needed; she was popular in society and being so exceptionally beautiful and accomplished, she had from time to time a number of suitors, to all of whom she would reply as she did to the Russian count. Besides, she would be violating the trust imposed in her, and as long as she remained an agent of the Red Cross, she would wed no man. The American Ambassador to the Russian Court had heard of Octavia's beauty and accomplishments, and of her refusing the Russian Count, and a number of other desirable suitors. He said to his wife, that they must seek the acquaintance of this wonderful American woman. They went to her hotel, sent in their card, and received a cordial greeting. Octavia said she was delighted to see any one from America, and especially the Ambassador and wife. They promised to call frequently, and that they would do all in their power to make her visit as pleasant as possible during her stay in the city. In Russia's gay capital, she had all that "wealth or beauty e'er gave," but there was a longing, which none of this would satisfy. She often thought of her home in America—of her dear uncle, of—yes, of her lover lawyer. Do what she may, she could not efface him from her memory. She resolved to return, and await an opportunity for service from the Red Cross. On the return voyage, her vessel was wrecked in a storm, half of the passengers perishing, she being among the saved, all of whom were carried to the nearest port, from whence they were forwarded to New York. She went out and spent a few days with Miss Mildred, who approved of her mission of mercy. She parted with her former governess with many regrets, and was soon caressing her uncle, in "Dixie's land." This was a joyful as well as sad meeting. Her mother had died during her absence, and there was a vacant chair which could never be filled. It took quite awhile to relate her experiences in Europe, of her refusal to be Countess ——, with wealth, ease, and all the pleasures of the Royal Court.

Simon told her that he was prouder of her now, than ever.

As was to be expected, her lover soon called, and while his correspondence with her in Europe was only of a friendly character, he had not despaired of making her his wife, if she ever returned. He renewed his suit with more fervor than ever, but to all his entreaties she would kindly but sadly say that were her environments or circumstances different, she would bestow her hand where her heart was already. His visits clandestinely made, were frequent. During her absence in Europe, he had been elected State's Attorney, a responsible and lucrative office, in which he had better opportunities to add to his already well earned fame.

After her return, she decided to write up her experiences in Europe minus the proposals, and publish them in one of the leading Northern journals. This, her first attempt at writing for the press, elicited favorable comment.

One day, while reading one of the latest novels, a messenger, nearly out of breath, came running in with the sad news that her uncle was dead. She hastened to the store, to find it too true. Her grief knew no bounds. The physician who had been called pronounced his trouble, apoplexy. She loved her uncle as she did her mother. Simon had gained the confidence of all classes, and had built up a large lucrative business. He was upright and honorable; just and fair in his dealings, and his death was a public loss. There was a large funeral procession, both white and black attending almost *en masse*.

In his will, Simon left everything to Octavia, making his book-keeper executor, without bond. Octavia requested him to immediately settle up the estate, turning all of Simon's property into money, which he easily did.

She also requested him to purchase two magnificent monuments for her mother's and uncle's grave.

Her lover continued his visits, offering what comfort he could to Octavia. Of course propriety forbade him mentioning matrimony. Octavia was indeed lonely now. Not a relative in the world that she knew of. How desolate! It is true, that troubles never come singly; as the day after her uncle's burial, she saw in the newspapers, notice of the death and burial of her former governess, Miss Mildred. In her loneliness, she would weep for hours at a time. But time heals all things, and in a few months, her grief was somewhat assuaged. She made up her mind to go North to live. At his next visit, she told the attorney of her intention. He then brought up the "tender subject," again, and made the plea of his life, telling her that she was alone in the world, and had no ties to bind her here, and to be happy the balance of his life, he would give up his office, his practice, and sever every tie that bound him here, and go with her anywhere on the globe, if, by so doing, he could make her his wife. She burst into tears because of her loneliness; tears, because of the barrier between them; and said that it would be best for them not to marry and that he would soon forget her, after her departure. He went away sorrowfully, resolving to resort to strategy. The next day, the city dailies contained the startling information, that State's Attorney ——, had resigned his office, wound up his affairs and would leave in a few days to make his home in one of the South American Republics. After seeing this, Octavia threw herself on her couch, and wept bitter, bitter tears. There is this difference in men and women when in trouble: the former, frequently resort to drink, while the latter resort to tears.

The attorney's masterpiece of strategy was successful.

Brutus, who was still doing the chores on the place, came in while Octavia was crying and said, "Miss Octay, what de matter?" she replied: "Nothing of consequence." He left, and she immediately recalled him and told him to come back in five or ten minutes, and take a note to State's Attorney ——. He left, saying, "Yes, miss." Brutus was soon back, when she sent the following note to the State's Attorney:

"Dear Mr. ——: I am miserable, oh, so miserable; please come to me at once! Octavia."

It is needless to say, he went, and was exulting over his successful strategy as he rang for admittance. She was waiting, and as he entered, she ran into his arms, saying: "Take me anywhere. I'll be your wife, regardless of all social laws."

To say there was a happy couple goes without saying.

In two days both left, the lawyer ostensibly for South America, and Octavia for New York City. Both, however, drew their money from the bank, and bought New York exchange.

They were quietly married in the metropolis of America. After marriage he laughingly told Octavia of the deception he had practiced upon her—that the notice in the city papers of his intended departure for South America was only a ruse to bring her to terms; that he had made no resignation, at that time, of his office, and that the notice was paid for as an advertisement. He said it was a two-edged sword, cutting both ways; at first, deceiving her, and then, the public, but with this difference: She was undeceived, while the public still thought he was by this time in the wilds of South America.

She embraced him, and amid a perfect shower of kisses, said:

"Let the public think as they please, the fact remains that you are my own dear husband, whom I love better than life itself, and I am glad, oh, so glad, that you took that means to bring me to terms. If you had not, I might have refused you from time to time, on account of the fraction of African blood that circulates in my veins, and you might, through spite, have married some woman that you did not love."

He admitted that there was much philosophy in what she had said, and, if she hadn't married him, that he might now have been in the Alabama River. He said that he didn't wonder at those Northern men killing themselves, and one another, about her.

Then saying, "My dear wife, let's dismiss all of those unpleasant things of the past, and talk about the future. Where shall we 'drive down stakes?'"

She said she would leave all that with him. While both of their means, put together, would make a fortune, and judiciously invested, would provide for them, the balance of their days, she was sure that a man of his caliber would want an active life, and would go where he could find it.

"Thank you," said he; "and that means one of the mining States of the West, which is comparatively new."

And there they went, and he prospered as he never did before. He located in the capital of the State, and soon was doing a good law practice.

Octavia became the center of attraction for a large coterie of friends, and if her husband had been of a jealous disposition, he might have shown it.

He was successively elected alderman, mayor of the city, representative and senator, in the State legislature, attorney-general and governor. In after years, when several children had blessed their union, they often spoke of their home in "Dixie's land;" of Octavia's many hairbreadth escapes; of the Northern tragedies on her account; of the many suitors who had received their mittens from her; of her Red Cross life; and last, but not least, of his successful strategy in bringing her to terms. Octavia admitted, shortly after marriage, that she deliberately ran off to Europe, knowing that if she remained, she would have to "marry him, to get rid of him."

They are now planning a visit to the old original home of Octavia, the Octoroon.

www.ingramcontent.com/pod-product-compliance
Lightning Source LLC
Chambersburg PA
CBHW071143250626

47159CB00006B/2278